GLIMPSES

A COLLECTION
OF SHORT STORIES

By Theresa Flerx

1

Glimpses

ISBN 978-0-615-54603-2

Introduction

Some of these stories contain violence, sexual content and vulgar language, flavored with a dark sense of humor.

I'm a fan of Stephen King, Dean Kountz and other writers of the horror, suspense and sci-fi genres. Glimpses is my contribution to these styles of storytelling.

All of my short stories are the fruitful bounty cultivated in the bizarre environment I wrote about in my life story, *Disequilibrium and the Multi-Faceted Crystal Ball*. You can't grow up in an insane household without developing a strange, tilted view of the world. This collection is the result of that tainted, fertile ground.

I've heard that it takes some authors years to write a book, but I wrote *Disequilibrium* in nine months. Glimpses, however, began in 2001. I wrote *Prisoner of Circumstance* that year, *The Life of a Dead Dog* in 2002. I began *Ghosts of Sandstone Manor* in 2004 but didn't finish until 2011. *Respite* is a fantasy I developed in 2008 after several traumatic events hit one right after the other. *Things Break* is an idea I expanded on in 2011 after a coworker greeted me daily with, "Break anything today?" I put *Forever Caged* on paper in 2011, but this story wrote itself in my mind in 2005 when I was a reporter visiting a similar hotel as in the tale.

I loved writing this type of book and look forward to writing more of them. Enjoy the emotional ride!

Contributions

I wish to thank Tracey Godby my friend and photographer for the picture on the cover. Visit www.whisperywillowphotography.com for more pictures.

I thank my mother for sharing a funny personal story to add to *Things Break*, and for giving me an idea for my next short story.

Thanks to Brittney Cassity, Debbie McDaniel, Wesley Wilson, Connie Roddas, Tracey, and those I'm sure I've forgotten, for reading my earlier drafts and encouraging me to finish this book, and Cary Bland.

Table of Contents

The Life of a Dead Dog 7

Respite 25

Prisoner of Circumstance 37

Ghosts of Sandstone Manor 75

Things Break 87

Forever Caged 95

The Life of a Dead Dog

This story was inspired by a radio news report about a dog that mysteriously recovered after being euthanized. Didn't he know he was supposed to be dead? I decided to take the tale several steps farther to tell the experiences this animal would have if this type of incident happened to the same dog again and again.

I gave The Life of a Dead Dog the honor of first position in this collection because, although it is not the creepiest one, it is a story that my fans really enjoy.

Susanne Moore had a busy life and it was about to get even busier. She was relocating to Chicago to start a promising career in advertising. This was the break she was hoping for while working as a waitress to put herself through college. Her dog Buddy just didn't fit into her plans.

He's just too big to live in my new apartment and I won't have time to walk him anyway. I love him and I'll miss him and all that, but I just won't have time to take care of him, Susanne rationalized.

She daydreamed about her new life as she drove along the small town streets. The dog was in the back seat, face stuck out of the window, tongue and ears flapping in the wind. He was enjoying this rare outing with his master, not knowing that it would be his last. She pulled into the driveway of the county pound, parked her Ford Focus, got out, opened the back door, grabbed Buddy by the collar and snapped on a leash saying, "Come on Big Boy, let's go." They walked inside and were greeted by Shelly, the vet tech."

"Hello, and who might this be?" Shelley asked as she reached down and took the black and brown, shaggy head into both hands.

"Hi, I'm Susanne Moore, this is Buddy. I called earlier about bringing him in."

"Oh, yes." After taking some information, Shelly asked, "Do you want to stay with him while the doctor euthanizes him?"

"No, I've got a lot of things to do. Thanks."

Buddy let out a small whimper as he watched his owner since puppyhood, walk out the door without a moment's hesitation.

The least she could have done was say goodbye to him, thought Shelly, as she led Buddy into the exam room to receive the shot that would stop his heart and end his life. *What a waste, he's such a good dog.*

The Town of Bloomberg Sanitation truck pulled up to the back door of the closed pound. Walt Deveraux climbed down from behind the wheel.

I hate coming here. I love animals and seeing all these dead pets gives me the creeps, blanks eyes staring at me, enough to give me nightmares, Walt thought.

He hooked up to the dumpster, operated the lift, and poured in the load as he tried to avoid watching the stiff bodies and matted fur spill into the bed of the truck. To Walt, this was the visual equivalent of nails on a chalkboard.

He got back into the truck and headed toward the town dump. He could see the scavenger birds circling long before he got there, and he could certainly smell the place long before he got there. The only good thing about coming here was that it meant his day was over. Soon his job would be over as well since he was closing in on retirement. Walt backed the truck up to the pile of debris, worked the lever, and let his cargo slide out of the tailgate. He shut down the engine and got out to make sure the bed was free of garbage, it was. As he started toward the front of the truck he heard a small throaty cry, *a gull?* He listened. He heard it again, and turned to see movement in the reeking trash heap, *just garbage settling.* Then he saw a large brown head emerge from the pile. It moved weakly then let out a pitiful moan.

Walt rushed over to it exclaiming, "My God, that dog's still alive! Easy big fella, it's alright now."

He lifted the animal up, carried him to the open driver side door and placed him down on the seat. He shoved The Dog over and slid in alongside. Walt kept an eye on The Dog as he drove the five miles back to the sanitation department.

"Hey there, you must have nine lives or something. It's a good thing I checked my truck bed." He patted the sticky, slimy head and said, "Whew you stink."

Some of the grogginess seemed to be leaving the dogs eyes as the truck pulled alongside Walt's personal pickup.

"Let's see if you can walk on your own now," Walt said as he pulled the creature, *Roger*, from the dump truck, "Yeah, that's it, I'll call you Roger. Like Roger Dodger, seeing how you dodged your own death." He chuckled, "I like that."

Roger could walk unaided, a little shaky, but he could walk. He slowly made his way to the pickup with the help of his new owner. He had some trouble getting up onto the seat so his master lifted up his rear end and pushed. While Walt clocked out, Roger Dodger waited in the truck, as a swirling fog slowly lifted from his brain.

The next stop was the pet store for dog supplies. Walt thought there was a vet counter there and knew it would be a good idea to have Roger examined before he took him home.

After an explanation of the situation, the vet preformed a quick checkup while Walt shopped for food, bowls, collar, leash and shampoo, you name it; he needed it now that he was a pet owner.

He paid for his purchases, deposited them into his truck, and went to the vet station to find out if his newest family member would be okay.

"Well, Mr. Deveraux, I think Roger is goin' to be just fine," Dr. Wood said, "It'll take some time for the drug to pass through his system so keep an eye on him tonight."

All told, Roger cost Walt $112.52 in less than two hours of dog ownership.

"You better survive after what I spent on you." Walt gave the smelly, crusty dog a hug, "A bath is now our top priority."

Walt lived alone on a small piece of land just outside of town until Roger came into his life. After Walt's retirement, they spent all their time together. They took long walks, watched the ducks swim on the pond, and even made a few cross-country trips in a rented R.V. They were the best of friends, inseparable, at least until the winter of '98.

The Winnebago, along with several other campers, was parked along the edge of the frozen

Massacre Lake. The snow was glittering with the glow of the rising sun when Walt opened the R.V. door.

"Come on Roger, we don't want to miss this beautiful sight. This is why we spent all that time driving."

Roger ran and soon sniffed out a rabbit's trail which led him along the lake shore. Walt carried a blue tackle box and fishing pole across the slippery sheet of ice. He was soon joined by Marilyn and Sal, who owned the Airstream parked alongside his.

"So Sal, I saw you out earlier this morning, did you catch any fish?"

"Nah, but then again, I wasn't really trying. You know, I was just hanging around, being lazy. Isn't that what vacation's all about?"

"You got that right, but it's awfully cold for just hanging out."

"Too cold for me that's for sure and I'm glad he didn't catch any fish. I'm tired of cleanin' 'em and I'm sick of eatin' 'em," Marilyn puffed out with a breath of frosted air.

Walt set about breaking the thick layer of ice that had hardened over his fishing hole during the night, while Sal did the same to his newly formed,

13

thin crust. They made general conversation until Walt started wondering about Roger.

"Oh, he's probably just sniffing around that girl beagle, down yonder," Sal said.

"Yeah, you're probably right," Walt said as he dropped his line into the frigid liquid.

Meanwhile, Roger had wandered along the far side of the lake, the thin side. This side was fed by a spring that was slightly warmer than the outside air so the ice hadn't solidified as hard as the rest. Walt glanced into the glare of the rising sun, just in time to see his dog drop down as chunks of silver rose up and swallowed his best friend. He raced across the ice as fast as his sliding boots could carry him, which wasn't very fast. He couldn't ice skate very well as a kid and now at 75 years old he looked absolutely doddering. When he got close to the place where Roger fell in, he dropped to his knees, then to his belly, and slide to the hole.

Sal, Marilyn, and several other campers had followed Walt to the rescue. Roger had floated several feet away from the original drop site, so it took some time to find him. He was under a thick slab of ice and had to be chopped out. When he was finally lifted to the surface five minutes later, he wasn't breathing and stiffened quickly when exposed to the low outside temperatures.

Another fisherman was an M.D. who tried several times to give mouth to snout resuscitation, but his attempts failed. One reason for failure was that the dog's mouth and nose had frozen shut. Dr. Jones pronounced Roger dead at 7:50 a.m.

Taking turns patting an obviously distraught Walt on the back, the campers and fisherman gave their condolences.

"Do you want me to take care of him for you, you know take him somewhere or sumthin'?" Sal asked.

"Well, I do need help getting 'im back to the camper, but I guess I'll figure out where to take 'im after that."

Two flannel clad young guys were left standing around after most of the people had wandered off, excitement over. They each took an end of the frozen creature and walked off toward Walt's Winnebago.

"You know, there's an animal control office out on Highway 50 that'll most likely dispose of his body for you. I'm sure you don't want to haul him home in that R.V. for two days. Wouldn't be very

15

healthy for you in a lot of ways," Dr. Jones told Walt, as they followed the two boys, along with Sal and his wife.

"That might be a good idea," Walt said as they reached his home on wheels, "And Doc thanks for all you did trying to save him, I really do appreciate it," tears now flooding his eyes.

"I know you do, but I wish I could have done more." and he held out his hand to be shaken.

Hugs, handshakes and goodbyes shared, Walt drove away, heading for Highway 50. He found the animal control building without any problem; it was 9:30 a.m. He got out of the recreation vehicle to read the hours printed on a "closed" sign hanging on the door. The hours for Saturday, which is what that day happened to be, were from noon till 6 p.m. Walt couldn't bear the thought of waiting there, looking at the site of his beloved Roger's lifeless body for two and a hours, so he decided to leave a note explaining what had occurred, and ask that the body be disposed of.

As he struggled to lift the animal he noticed that some of the stiffness had gone, but realized the dog had been in a warm vehicle for a while and chalked it up to that. He laid the animal down gently,

16

almost reverently. He patted Roger's head, said his final goodbye and walked away to drive the long hours back home to Bloomberg with a deep sadness in his soul.

The sunshine illuminated The Dog, making the icy fur thaw and glisten. His body warmed. His temperature rose. Then his chest rose. A breath? Yes, a breath. And then another. His head lifted, and then his body. He looked around, found no one there and went to search for Walt.

At 11:30 a.m. Bonnie, the receptionist arrived to open the animal control office. She took the note from the door and read it, but there was no dog in sight. She shrugged and went inside to get ready for the day.

Rachael Long realized she hadn't heard a peep out of Maggie, her 4-year-old who was in the backyard building a snowman. Their house was on a farm, so Rachael wasn't worried about anyone bothering the little girl. She was free to wander, at least as long as she stayed within the fence. But, Maggie was unusually quiet, probably up to no good. Rachael found her in the yard, but not alone. The tiny child had her arms around a massive dog, trying to lead it to the garage.

"Maggie, where did that come from?"

"The woods, Mom. He's all wet, see?"

The Dog was indeed wet. The black and brown shaggy creature was shaking himself, spraying droplets in an arc. Rachael sent Maggie into the house for a towel and then blotted him dry.

"Can I keep him, Mom, please?" little hands together as if in prayer.

"We'll see what your father says when he gets home. But, you know if he chases the cows we can't keep him."

"He won't Mom, I promise."

He didn't, so Mom and Dad agreed he could stay. They called him Mack. Mack was a good source of entertainment for Maggie. She hooked him up to a pony cart, he was used as a neck cushion while watching T.V., and he pulled her along on ice skates in the winter. He often left dirty paw prints on her bedspread. As much as Rachael tried to dissuade him, she couldn't keep him from climbing in bed with the girl, but it was a small price to pay for the cheer he brought to the family.

Maggie was an only child and living in the middle of nowhere could get lonely, but not with Mack around. He heard all of the girl's life's problems, especially during her preteen years. She cried into his fur about many boy troubles. His eyes looked up at her adoringly, he worshiped her, and she him. He was the best friend one could ever hope for.

During his yearly check up, the vet suggested Mack have his teeth cleaned. It should have been done sooner, but the Long's barely had enough money to get their teeth cleaned, so it was put off as long as possible. Now, for health reasons it was time. When Dr. Reese administered the anesthesia, Mack's heart stopped. Maybe it was because of his previous medical history, who knows, but for whatever the reason, his heart stopped. The vet tried several desperate attempts to get it started again, but failed. He had to give the family the sad news.

Mack's body was placed in a wooden box outside of the clinic; it was to be picked up in the morning before the office opened. Will Long, his wife Rachael and daughter Maggie planned to bury Mack in the yard with a hand carved wooden cross marking the grave, so the dog would be close to his grieving owner. Although, Maggie was raised on a farm and had seen many animals die, the loss of her pet was unbearable.

With funeral plans made, Will arrived at the clinic in the morning to find the wooden box empty, the lid leaning against the side. There was no sign of the deceased. Nothing was discovered during a search of the area, and it was speculated that a mountain lion may have dragged the body into the woods. A memorial service would have to do.

Ed Samms drove his battered Jeep Wrangler down Rural Route 120 with the top down. He was pushing the buttons on his radio trying to find a good song. He almost hit the big black and brown dog crossing the road, but slowed down and swerved in time to avoid hitting it.

"Stupid dog," He stopped and got out, "Hey, what the hell ya' doin'!"

The Dog wasn't used to being yelled at, so he just stood there and wagged his tail in response. "Well you are dumb, ain't ya? Git over here."

The Dog walked over, tail still wagging, tongue hanging out.

"You want to go home with me, Stupid?"

Ed and Stupid leaped into the Jeep, which then left noxious, yellow-brown fog in its wake.

Ed's house was as battered as the vehicle he drove, and was located in the middle of the town of Sutton. It had belonged to his mother until her death two years ago, it hadn't been cleaned since, junk was piled everywhere, inside and out.

Stupid found his new home in the yard, wedged between an oven and a stack of old plastic milk crates, fence boards slanting across them serving as a very crude dog shelter which fell a little short of ASPCA standards. He was tied to the chain link fence behind this jumbled mess. An old hub cap was used for water, when it was filled; his diet consisted of table scraps, when they were available. What was available though, was abuse, plenty of it.

Stupid was always happy to see Ed, so he wagged his tail since it got lonely in the yard all day, and sometimes he brought him food, but not today.

"Hey, what are you so happy about, huh?" These words were followed by a swift kick to the side.

Stupid yelped.

"I work with pain in the ass people all day; I don't feel like coming home to look at your ignorant face" with another kick of the heavy work boots.

Yelp!

Ed picked up a short piece of angle iron from the ground and swung it at Stupid. He cracked the cringing beast between the ears. The dog fell to the ground, his legs kicking as if running. Then they slowed. Then they stopped moving altogether.

"Damn! I think I killed my dog," a nervous giggle came out with this statement, "He was a pain in the ass anyway."

Ed loaded the body and a shovel into his Wrangler and drove about one mile out of town. He exited the country road onto a dirt road that crossed some farm land. After digging a shallow grave he dropped the sack of fur that had once been a dog, into the hole and covered it over.

Winifred Kellogg enjoyed sitting on her back porch in the evening, looking out at the farmland. Her home was technically in the city of Winsted, but it bordered the countryside, so it seemed like country to her, especially in the back of the house. As the elderly woman took in the fresh air at twilight she saw a shape crossing the field, her eyesight wasn't what it used to be, so she couldn't make out what it was at first. When it got closer to her porch, she realized it was a dog. It was covered in mud and probably weighed twenty pounds less than it should.

"Oh, my goodness! Look at that." She rose to her feet and called The Dog to her. He came slowly; head down, a little unsure, but still wagging his tail. "Oh, you must be starving. I don't have any dog food, maybe cat food will do for now."

She feed him what she had, he devoured it. She hosed him down as best she could manage with arthritic hands. That first night she made him a bed of her handmade quilts, but somehow he made his way onto her bed, and that is where he slept every night after that. Trooper became a faithful companion and watchdog.

On a cold December night two years later, 90-year-old Winifred, bundled up in the quilts she was known for, sighed out her last breath. It was a peaceful passing after a long and satisfying life. Trooper lay beside her. He rested his black, brown and gray muzzle on her silent chest and breathed a sigh of his own. It too, was his last. For the most part, he also had a long and satisfying life.

Respite

This story is a personal favorite. It is a tale that leans toward sci-fi about an innovative sleep therapy. The idea for Respite developed as I was handling some of the darkest years of my life. I often wished there was a stress treatment that would allow me to sleep away my troubles.

"Huh," Kevin grunted. *I could use a long rest*, he thought. The 15-year veteran of the Chicago Police Department had recently suffered the most traumatic experience of his lifetime.

Although he fought against it, and tried hard to concentrate on the newspaper in front of him, the memories came flooding back, back to the apartment house on Washington Street.

An investigation had led Detective Kevin Wilcox and his partner of 8 years, Hank Melvern, to the run-down apartment building after a confidential

26

informant told them it was the source of most of the drugs in the area. It was not an actual drug lab, "Butch" had said. If it had been the investigators would have brought back-up and a haz-mat team with them. This was just a distribution center for meth, pot, oxycodone, and pretty much any type of illicit drug on the market. Wilcox and Melvern went to the location as a preliminary scouting trip, just to get a sense of whether the informant's story was anything close to the truth.

The chatter of playing kids could be heard as soon as the detectives walked into the entrance hall of the complex. They didn't see the three boys until they climbed to the top of the second floor stairway. Since they were both dressed in street clothes, the investigators made an enormous error by assuming they wouldn't be recognized as the police. They were wrong. Maybe children raised within a criminal environment develop an intuition for any threat to their family unit, no matter how dysfunctional, Wilcox later reasoned.

"Cops," the smallest boy shouted.

The trio ran for an opened door on the right situated halfway down a long corridor. The officers ran to catch the door before there was time to get it closed and locked. Both had un-holstered their weapons. Melvern arrived first and got a foot between the door and jam before it was slammed against his boot. He pushed the door open just as a deafening sound split the air. *An explosion. No. A shotgun blast.*

Melvern was thrown back across the hall and against the opposite wall. Wilcox had been right on his heels, but was unharmed. He cautiously peered into the room and saw a human shape sprawled on its back with the gun pointing to the ceiling, apparently having been pushed to the floor with the firearm's powerful force. As the form sat upright it began to aim the weapon in his direction. Wilcox raised his hand and fired a single shot into the person seated on the floor before him. It wasn't until he took the shotgun from the now-dead shooter's hands that he realized it was one of the boys who had been playing in the hall not two minutes before the incident. After simultaneously radioing for help, and determining the other two kids had climbed down a fire escape to the alley below, the detective returned to his partner's side. Wilcox took Melvern's bloody hand in his and spoke softly to his best friend.

"Remember how drunk I got at your wedding? Fine best man I turned out to be, huh. 'Member Molly's first Easter dress? How she got chocolate all over it? She got chocolate all over everything. 'Member Matt's first home run? That was great. That's all you talked about for weeks."

Wilcox tried to lead his partner down a trail of happy family memories as he watched the blood and life drain out of his buddy's body.

"Yeah, I sure could use a rest," Kevin said as he sat in his kitchen and held the morning paper.

"...drained? Mentally exhausted? A long rest can help you heal! The Gilbertson Clinic..."

"I wonder if they can provide a peaceful rest," Linda asked herself, as she listened to the radio commercial during her drive to work.

Maybe a long rest is what she needs. Since all of the physical pain was gone, maybe a rest at the clinic will heal the emotional wounds.

Linda MacCarty was really Ann Bennett from Wildwood, New Jersey. She had fled her seaside town a year ago last month. She was fleeing to escape her husband Bob whose hobby, it seemed, was to pick fights with her and then slam her up against the wall. He wasn't always like that but his other hobbies began to take a toll on him and eventually her. Gambling and drinking in Atlantic City were his other pleasures. Poker was a pleasure, until his luck changed anyway.

It was fun for both of them at first. Bob would come home on Friday nights all excited. Sometimes he would have complimentary tickets for a show. He watched the entertainment with her occasionally, but after a while his only interest was playing poker. Ann didn't mind in the beginning. Bob was good at it and won quite often. Sometimes he would buy her something special with his winnings; he did that more after he started beating her, though.

Bob had threatened to have her killed if she left him, and he had the type of friends who could back up his threat. But she knew if she stayed it was

29

her soul that would die, and that she couldn't live with. She developed the motto - "I would die for Bob, but I won't allow him to kill me." She meant "to kill" her in an emotional sense as well as the physical one.

After a few years, her husband stopped inviting her to a night at the casinos. Ann suspected he had met someone else, and that this woman now accompanied him. Around this time she started to make her escape plan. After Bob came home drunk and passed out, Ann removed the bills and loose change from his pockets, placed this bounty in a shoe box and stashed the box above the ceiling tiles in the closet. Her husband didn't miss this cash. It was the money he used to tip the dealers and waitresses. Ann thought he probably got so drunk he didn't realize how much he had handed out. The money added up to a sizable amount in 18 months.

Ann packed an overnight bag one Friday night, took a bus to Philadelphia, a train to Baltimore, a cab to D. C. and then boarded another train headed for Fort Lauderdale. It was in Florida that she felt safe enough to buy a plane ticket to Chicago. She climbed aboard the jet as Ann Bennett, but debarked as Linda MacCarty.

Linda didn't know a soul in Illinois and this gave her a sense of freedom. But the act of putting her former life behind her, creating a fictional past, assuming a new identity, starting a job, planning a future (not to mention looking over her shoulder to make sure her past didn't sneak up on her) were taking a toll on her health. Nothing seemed more like heaven then the thought of an extended rest.

"....can help you heal! The trained staff at the Gilbertson Clinic can provide..."

Charlie Dunbar watched the white lab-coated man on his T.V. screen and tried to focus on the message he was hearing. "...that peaceful rest..."

Concentrating on the world around him had been a hard feat to accomplish ever since he lost his wife Margaret. She had lived a long life, but not a healthy one. The last four years had been horrendous. Four-and-a-half years ago, Margie had been diagnosed with skin cancer. It started in a mole on the side of her neck. A mole she had all of her life.

Charlie and Margie believed the cancer had been completely removed, but a spot soon appeared in the same location. This growth was also removed. And again it grew back. From there it metastasized to the lymph nodes and slowly sapped the verve and vigor out of his precious wife of 24 years.

It had gotten to the point where he would go to bed at night not knowing whether she would be alive or dead in the morning. If she were dead, he imagined, he would wonder how long he had slept beside her lifeless body. Or whether she had tried to wake him to say goodbye, and he had slept right through her passing. Those thoughts he couldn't bear.

As it were, she faded away in the hospital with Charlie sitting by her side. Margaret was drugged so heavily by then she didn't really know what was going on. Thank heaven for small favors.

Pictures lined the walls of the Dunbar home. Reminders of the life they lived together. Charlie and Margie had met in junior high. He looked at a photo of a summer's night stroll, and heard crickets. Charlie fishing, looking over his shoulder as Margaret snapped the shot. He saw her smile. Swirls of white fill the frame of their wedding day dance. He could feel her warmth. He studied a picture of him sitting beside his wife with an hour old Sara in his arms. He could smell the baby's scent.

"I am so tired," Charlie sighed.

"My name is Doctor Wayne Gilbertson," he told the class of residents seated in the lecture hall of the clinic.

"I'm sure you remember what I'm about to tell you from first year med school, but I must remind those of you who may have forgotten. Now, I know learning is a stressful process but I am all about relieving stress, not adding to it." Chuckles filled the hall. "Non-rapid eye movement sleep is one without dreams. It is a peaceful sleep, with a slow rate of breathing, heart rate and lower blood pressure. Most of our night's sleep is spent in this state, about 80% actually. From my extensive research in sleep science, I've discovered dreams can add to trauma by allowing the mind to create distortions of reality, often exacerbating the problem, and compounding the emotional pain by causing a person to relive the traumatic experience. I have come to the conclusion that by preventing dreams and nightmares, medical science can allow the mind to rest and repair itself. I have developed a method of placing a patient into a dreamless state and keeping them there for as long as is necessary to heal the mind and body, and, hopefully the soul."

Gilbertson led the group of residents onto the balcony overlooking the barely lit sleep lab. Motionless human figures could be seen inside clear tubes set in rows three deep and four wide.

"Before being considered for the clinic, the patients must have a psychiatric evaluation to give me a better understanding of the stress each one has suffered. I use these evals to determine the length of time each patient must remain in the sleep chambers," Gilbertson explained. "Serious trauma victims may heal in a matter of weeks. A trauma of major significance can require as much as six months before the patient feels relief."

The doctor led the residents down to the lab, and escorted them among the tubes filled with sleeping people. Posters colored in calming shades of blues and greens lined the cream painted walls. The one on the left wall featured the quote, "Sleep: the golden chain that ties health and our bodies together," written by Thomas Dekker. "Rest has cured more people than all the medicine in the

33

world," by Harold J. Reilly, hung on the wall at the opposite side of the room.

"The breathing of a person in the first two stages of non-REM sleep is slower than when awake. In the second two stages, slow-wave or delta sleep occurs, where the respiration slows down even further," Gilbertson said. "It is in the delta sleep stage that we keep the patients for the duration of their treatment. This is accomplished by administering tryptophan and calcium along with a specially prepared serum through an IV drip. Calcium provides a calming effect and aids the tryptophan in helping the brain produce the sleep inducing hormone melatonin. Lavender, which also aids in the production of melatonin, is pumped in with oxygen. Regular physical therapy is a must to prevent atrophy of muscle tissue," the doctor continued.

The group left the lab and entered a private room which was so dark they could hardly make out the body lying in a tube surrounded by nurses and technicians. The residents watched intently as Dr. Gilbertson's staff began to awaken the man in the glass cylinder. The lights began to brighten ever so slowly to replicate the rising sun.

"As the lighting is increased, the IV drip is slowly decreased. Here at the clinic we are trying to simulate the natural rise of the sun and the body's reaction to it. With the break of dawn, the shine of sunlight on the eyes causes the production of melatonin to slow down. As the IV of serum, calcium and tryptophan are decreased, an injection of CoEnzyme Q10 and vitamin E is given to prevent a heart attack from the rising heart rate and blood pressure which accompanies the wakeful state," Gilbertson explained.

After the lid of the tube was raised, Charlie Dunbar slowly sat up.

"If I hadn't tried it myself, I wouldn't have believed it. I was so desperate for some relief after the loss of my wife, Margaret, that I thought it was worth a try. After two weeks at The Gilbertson Clinic, I have never felt so peaceful." Charlie told the audience of the late night infomercial.

While wearing a disguise and speaking into a voice distortion system, Linda MacCarty told the bleary-eyed insomniacs, "My long rest at The Gilbertson Clinic has allowed me to more effectively move on with my life. I now feel confident in who I am, and where I am headed."

"My nightmares are over. My anxiety has stopped. The other symptoms of the post traumatic stress I suffered after the murder of my partner and the horrible incident afterward have ended since my three month's stay at The Gilbertson Clinic. I have been cleared to return to my job at the Chicago Police Department. I highly recommend the sleep treatment." Detective Kevin Wilcox said.

Prisoner of Circumstance

When I was in kindergarten, my family lived to the right of the couple this story is very loosely based on. I set Prisoner of Circumstance in my old neighborhood and patterned Anna and Melvin Walsh after the couple who lived to the left of my home. Although I was not raised in a violent household, Amy has a lot of my traits and sense of humor.

These things weren't discussed in 1964. They weren't anyone else's business. It was personal. A marital issue. It happened all the time, no big surprise, unless it happens the way it did with Harry Tobias.

Many families lived on Marks Street, a narrow, dead-end street in the "City of Brotherly Love." But, they weren't all loving families. Not all brothers loved their brothers, not all fathers loved their children. And, as it was in Harry's case, not all wives loved their husbands. Harry's wife Marcia was in fact downright cruel. What went on behind their closed door was not a loving story.

Marcia liked Friday's. It was her happy day. At least in the early part of it when the house was quiet, the day stretched out before her, and the beer was fresh out of the tap. She put her feet up on the ottoman and took a long drink and laughed.

"As my grandmother used to say, 'my tongue was hanging out for that sip of beer.' "

She just sat there in the living room of the only home she'd ever known. This was her castle and she ruled it with an iron fist. Her parents willed it to her and she owned it for the past 14 years.

Marcia was born upstairs in the room she now shared with that weenie of a husband.

One of these days I'm going to get myself a real man. Maybe even become a career woman, she thought.

She had worked at the Navy Yard while Harry was away during the war, and at the chocolate factory before Amy was born. She could work again if it was something worthy of her. She didn't have any particular skills or talents, but she had no doubt that anyone would be lucky to have her as an employee. She could be a secretary, or phone operator, or an assistant to the president of a corporation. She dreamed away her morning that way as she slowly absorbed the alcohol into her bloodstream, dreaming nice, pleasant thoughts. She even dozed off a few times.

At noon, she watched her shows and dreamed about the glamorous lives the soap stars lived. By mid afternoon, her internal organs thoroughly soaked in booze, she traveled into the dark thoughts. How if she hadn't wasted all her precious years waiting for Harry Tobias and then later raising that kid of his, then maybe she could be Somebody. She married Harry because he was a polite, gentle man. He was so handsome the first time she saw him wearing his military uniform.

They were at a USO dance at St. Michael's Church. She was all dolled up and *looked pretty good if I do say so myself.* Her body was much nicer in those days, *You can see what carrying that brat, Amy, for nine months did to me* (not to mention cheese steaks, hoagies and all the beers over a lifetime. But, of course, Marcia couldn't admit to that). All the men wanted to dance with her, stood in line in fact.

She was leaning against the wall talking to her cousin, Bea, when Harry caught her eye. He was smoking a cigarette and joking with a few Marine buddies. There was chemistry at first sight, but then again arsenic is a chemical, isn't it? They dated for a few months and got married right before he shipped out for the South Pacific.

When he was overseas, she waited for him for a while, but then got sort of lonely. She started flirting with the sailors at work and hung out at the local bars. There weren't a lot of men left at home, but there were a few that couldn't past the physical for some reason or another. It wasn't hard to gain sympathy for a lonely woman waiting for her husband to return home. She found many a man willing to keep her company, both married and unmarried. Maybe she should have run away with one instead of waiting for poor, simpering Harry. And people called him a hero, *if he was such a hero, he wouldn't have surrendered, he'd of fought to the death*, swam through her head, as she grew increasingly mean throughout the day. It would be a long time before she saw him again. He returned home right before Christmas of 1945. Well, not him exactly, a *pathetic shell of him, was more like it. What a Christmas present he was*, ran though her sick mind.

In late afternoon, Marcia stumbled into the kitchen intending to make supper. Amy and Harry would be home soon, complaining about being hungry. She made it as far as the kitchen table, where she swayed, sat down and got lost in a stupor. She sat that way for an hour when she was brought around by that man sneaking into the room, babbling about going out to eat or something.

Harry felt the sense of dread rise before he left McMartin's Printing Company where he worked as a deliverer of paper goods for the past 15 years. It was Friday, the day after Baron's Distributer's made its stop at his house to drop off Marcia's weekly keg of beer. That meant Marcia would have had all day to drink like this was the last beer left on earth and it was all hers. Another gut-wrenching event was in store.

He made the short drive home as long as he possibly could, making a stop that he really didn't need to make, trying to postpone the inevitable. Bobby McDaniel was behind the counter of the small neighborhood corner store.

"Hey Bob, how 'bout a pack of Chesterfields," Harry said.

Bobby reached to the rack behind him and threw a pack to the counter as he said, "Sure, that'll be seventy-five cents."

Harry handed the clerk the exact change, complaining for the hundredth time, "Seventy-five cents. When they get to be a dollar, I'm quittin'. "

When he arrived home he was greeted by a ray of sunshine that was trying to stay one step ahead of a storm, and that was his 8-year-old daughter, Amy, the only good thing his marriage ever produced. He felt guilt sweep over him once again. Storms should never have to pass through this little angel's life. She was sitting on the gray marble steps in front of his house, wearing her blue and white polka-dotted dress with white shoes. Still in her school clothes, Harry realized.

"Whatcha doin' sittin' out here all by yourself?" he asked.

She looked back over her shoulder to the front door as she said "I didn't want to bother Mommy.

"Well let's just go on in and get you into some comfortable clothes and see what Mommy's up to," as if he couldn't already guess.

Harry opened the unlocked door and led is daughter in by the hand, keeping her close. There wasn't much light in the living room because the yellowed shades that were hanging on the two front windows were still closed. Marcia liked it dark while she drank, "Added to the ambience," she claimed. All was quiet, for now. His wife was probably in the kitchen.

"Go on upstairs and change now, Sweetie." Amy's room was as good a place as any to keep her out of the line of fire.

She climbed the stairs on tiptoe trying to keep the treads from squeaking as Harry ventured into the kitchen at the back of the house. He was putting on a cool exterior while steeling himself for a typical Friday night. *Keep a positive attitude*, he thought, *maybe things will be different tonight. People can change, can't they?*

Marcia was sitting at the table they had bought right before Amy was born. It was red with bands of white at either rounded end, wrapped in aluminum trim, and there were red teapots printed on the white stripes. The set came with four aluminum, red vinyl-cushioned chairs. She was staring out the window into the backyard. *She doesn't look happy, oh, not at all. But still, looks can be deceiving. Take a chance, see how she is,* he thought.

"Hello, Marcia, how ya doin'? It's a nice day out. So nice that Amy was sittin' outside on the steps enjoyin' it. How'd you like to go for a short walk before dinner, or maybe we could even go to Edie's Seafood House for somethin' to eat tonight, seein' that it's Friday and all?"

"Seafood? Is that what you want, huh, seafood?" her voice rose with each syllable, "We're gonna walk down to Edie's and get seafood, are we?"

She was a big woman and getting bigger as she started to stand. Harry's heart sank. Any hope for

44

a change from the usual was washed out of him. *Here we go again.*

"Are you made of money? Did you win the lott'ry? Mr. Rich Guy wants to go to Edie's for seafood."

She lit another cigarette even though there was one still smoldering in the ashtray.

"Well... okay... then we can just stay here and...I don't know..." He was backing away, trying to avoid being pinned against the refrigerator, as she came slowly toward him, cigarette aimed at his right cheek.

"Marcia, no. I'm sorry."

He squirmed out of his precarious position and scooted past her meaty right arm as the glowing coal seared into the tip of his earlobe.

"You are sorry. A sorry excuse for a man," venom dripped from her words, as she reached for the coffee cup that was hanging from a mug tree on the counter. She hurled it and the white porcelain splintered against the wall, a chip flying free and nicking Harry's neck.

"Please, Marcia... Amy's just upstairs, you'll upset her," not quite a whimper, but close.

"You're the one that upsets her, not me. You, with your crazy talk 'bout going out ta dinner. Given' her ideas." she said then snapped.

Harry moved into the dining room, trying to avoid the brunt of his wife's fury. *If I can just stay moving she'll lose interest or get tired and pass out.* She picked up one of the walnut chairs and swung, breaking it against the man's left shoulder. He cried out and fell to the floor. *I can handle this, I've been to war, I survived a POW camp,* and he did what he did then, he went into his private emotional storm shelter, where he could still hear the destruction and devastation above him, but he didn't let it in. He dealt with the aftermath later, when the storm was over. Did his clean-up and repairs afterward, so to speak. For now there was nothing to do but wait. And he curled into a ball and took the punches and kicks, and waited for it to be over.

Amy had been upstairs, but not anymore. When she heard the tone of her parents conversation, she grabbed the first thing she could find to wear, a pair of pink peddle-pushers, and a green flowered top, dressed as quickly as possible, and headed for the stairs. She was on the steps when the cup hit the wall, and out the door she went.

She didn't go immediately next door to the Walshes. She waited outside for a little while, feeling guilty for not staying for her father, but she knew instinctively that the best way for her to help was to stay out of the way. She stared at the hopscotch grid that she and Carlie had chalked in front of the house back in August. Her friend came over often during the summer vacation when she visited her grandparents down the street, but she saw her rarely while school was in session and she missed her, especially, during days like this. The two friends would sit out in the backyard of Carlie's Granmom and play with their Barbies or board games, savoring the warmth and quiet. Sometimes they would play in the street, only moving to the sidewalk when the occasional neighbor drove down the block. There was a six foot high, brick wall at the end of the street, separating the residences from the railroad tracks. The old people told stories of how they would walk the tracks looking for loose coal to use for heat during the Depression. Amy loved this place most of the time. If it wasn't for that woman in there beating up on her Dad, she'd love it even more. Nostalgia time was interrupted abruptly by a huge crash and a pain riddled scream, shaking Amy to the core. She could no longer contain her tears as she turned to knock on her sanctuary door.

Harry shouldn't have to suffer like this again. He'd suffered enough during the Death March and at The Camp. Starvation, disease, and lack of medicine and ammo prevented them from mounting a counter attack, forcing their surrender. He saw so many in his troop die right before his eyes from malaria and at the hands of the Japanese. He watched, weak and helpless, as his best buddy, Rob, was beheaded. He was so sick on several occasions that he nearly died. What kept him fighting for his life then was the thought that a beautiful and loving wife was waiting for him at home. He often reminisced about the night they met. She was standing there in a dark blue dress and black silk stockings, the lights sparkling in her brown hair and eyes. He was shy but approached her anyway, at the goading of his friends. He asked her to dance, and they were pretty good together. They went on their first date the following Saturday and started seeing each other as much as possible before he shipped out. The day he got his orders they were married. The rest, as they say, is history.

There was a frantic knock on the door of 1912 Marks Street, a two story, brick, row home in the middle of the block. Anna Walsh answered the door and found a barefoot Amy Tobias there with tears streaming down her face. Anna let her in. She didn't ask what was wrong, she didn't have to. This wasn't the first time Amy came, crying, to her door and she was sure it wouldn't be the last. She was expecting the knock ever since she heard the first piece of glass crash against the adjoining wall that separated her home from the Tobias'. Amy had been coming to her home since she was about 4, whenever her parents fought.

Anna brushed back the stray hairs that had fallen from its black and gray streaked bun and took care of Amy the way she always did. She turned on the T.V., tuned it to channel three for after school cartoons, turned the volume up really loud, sat the thin, blonde child in front of it, and went to the small kitchen for a peanut butter sandwich and milk. Neither Anna nor her husband Melvin ate peanut butter, but it was always on hand for Amy. Melvin thought peanut butter was for kids and since the Walshes were childless, and in their mid 50's, that little girl was the only reason there was peanut butter in their house.

Anna adored Amy and knew the situation next door was no way to raise a kid. She wanted to keep her but she knew that when the latest rumble was over her father would come back to get her as if nothing had happened. She sighed and took the snacks into the living room.

She laid the plate and glass on the coffee table and said, "Here, Hon, have something to eat while you watch your show." This was greeted with the most heart-melting smile imaginable and a small, "Thank you."

Amy sat on the floor behind the table with her back against the sofa and tentatively ate her snack, chewing slowly and washing it down with milk. Even though the T.V. was too loud, and she didn't want to hear, she was alternately trying to hear what was going on next door, and trying to ignore it. She was worried. Not for herself, she always felt safe here. She was worried about her father. He was no match for her mother. That woman was just so big. He was so gentle. When she was hurt, or sad, or scared it was Dad she ran to, or here. Here she felt safe.

But Harry's safety was another issue. The pummeling and howling shrieks wound down slowly and he knew Marcia was growing tired, or bored (he was never sure which,) and this round was coming to an end. When it stopped, he lay there for a few minutes, making sure she was finished and not just faking him out. The next feeling Marcia had was of being tired, so she lay down on the couch and went to sleep. That was 23 minutes after Harry led their daughter into the house.

Amy finished her sandwich and watched Magila Gorilla. She liked this cartoon and even had the coloring book, but she kept straining her ears to hear what was going on at her house. She couldn't tell. Was it better to hear something, or nothing? If she could hear voices or sounds she would know everyone was still alive, but if it were quiet was the worst over, or just beginning? Who knew?

"Amy, how's it going in school?" Anna asked.

"It's okay. I got an A on my science fair project, it was about the circ'latory system, you know, the veins and art'ries, and stuff. I drew them in red and blue. I even got a blue ribbon," Amy beamed.

"Well, good for you! I'm so proud of you! You'll have to show me the drawing and ribbon some time."

"Daddy was proud, too. I hung the ribbon on the mirror in my room."

Anna noticed there was no mention of what her mother thought of any of this, or that Amy hadn't said anything about her parents coming to the science fair to watch her do the presentation. If she had known about it, she and Melvin would have gone there to watch.

That reminded her, "Melvin will be home soon, would you like to help me make dinner? I'm making blue fish, french fries and a salad, you can help me bread the fish, if you want. I hope you like blue fish. Do you?"

"I've had it before, it's good," Amy answered, "Carlie's Pop Pop catches them in the ocean and brings them home in his trunk full 'a ice."

"Well, that's just where I got this fish, from Carlie's Pop Pop," Anna said as she stood to go into the kitchen. Amy followed, still listening to the walls, but she didn't hear a sound. Good? Bad? She was still tense but beginning to relax a little with the thought of having something to do.

When Harry heard the coach springs squeak as his wife lay down, he uncurled himself and headed upstairs to clear his head and assess the damage. He checked his shoulder where she cracked him a good one and then his ribs. Aside from hurting like hell, the wounds appeared to be superficial, nothing broken. *Thank God, no trip to the hospital this time. I'm running out of excuses*, he thought. He wiped the blood from his neck and applied a Band-Aid, then put some burn ointment on his ear. An ache was starting to radiate from the back of his head. He pressed his hand to the spot and felt tenderness there.

He wandered into Amy's room, sighed, lay down on her bed, wrapped his arm around a pink, stuffed pony, breathed in the scent of her, and wept. He lay like that for a time, and like always, tried to figure a way out of all this. He knew that if he left he would never see his little girl again. Marcia would never allow it, and the only reason she would keep her was for spite, certainly not for love. He didn't know if she were capable of love. He would lose his will to live without Amy. Without resolving his problem, he gathered his strength to go next door and pick up his daughter; he knew she would be worried.

He checked on Marcia, as he walked down the steps, she was still out cold, and knowing by experience, that was the way she would stay until morning. Thank God for small favors.

Anna reached into the refrigerator and took out an egg and the salad vegetables and laid them on the table. She took out bowls, plates, and cornmeal from the cabinets above the counter. She broke the egg on the edge of a bowl, and it slithered in. After whisking it with a fork, she set the bowl in front of Amy, along with the bag of cornmeal.

"Let's wash our hands and get started." That completed, "Now pour some of the cornmeal onto that plate, dip the fish in egg and then the meal, just like this, okay?"

"Okay. It looks messy, but fun," Amy's typical enthusiasm appeared.

Anna left the little one with that task and started chopping the salad vegetables, "It's nice havin' someone keep me company in the kitchen. Thank you for helping."

"No problem, I like it." Her fingers were plastered with egg and cornmeal. Her mind and body was so occupied with her chore that she didn't think about the trouble at her own house, until there was a knock at the door, *Dad.* She inhaled deeply, not realizing until that moment that she had been partially holding her breath.

Anna stopped slicing and went to open the door. There stood Harry with a sheepish look on his face, "Hi, Anna, I'm sorry to bother you, but I'm looking for Amy, is she here?" After quickly washing her hands, Amy came running.

"She was helping me with dinner. Would you and Amy like to stay and eat with us?" Anna replied, with no mention of the reason for Amy being there in the first place, but that was the usual routine.

"No, thank you, we'll just be on our way. Come on, Sunshine. Tell Anna thank you."

"Thank you. 'Bye now." Not looking at Anna, but her father, doing a quick, visual inspection. Not stopping at the bandage and burn, but searching for more.

"You're welcome. Goodbye." *Well, I'm glad I gave her that sandwich because I'm sure that bitch didn't make dinner*, Anna thought as she closed the door.

Harry led Amy cautiously through the front door much like he had done hours before, just in case the Beast was awake. But he didn't have to worry; she was still out, snoring away. They went upstairs. There was a T.V. in his and Marcia's bedroom, and since he knew that she wouldn't be coming up, he and Amy would have some peace and quiet.

"Why don't you get some toys out of your room and bring them in here?" he suggested.

"Be right back," as she scooted across the hall.

She grabbed some paper dolls with clothes and her Candy Land game. Sometimes her Dad played it with her on nights like this. She carried them back into the big room and laid them on the bed, then climbed up beside her father. They played Candy Land for a while, Amy won all three games.

Harry and Amy then watched television until they fell asleep from the exhaustion built up by the tension of the day.

At 6:15, Melvin arrived home, after first stopping to cash his paycheck from Wilford Plastics Factory. He was carrying a cheap version of a large Barbie dressed in layers upon layers of frilly purple lace. He handed it to Anna.

"Here, I bought this for Amy. Margaret from work makes these dresses for these dolls, and I thought she might like it."

"Oh, how cute, she'll love it. She was here today." She sighed

"Really? How bad was he this time?" Melvin didn't seem surprised as he questioned his wife.

"Nothing too bad that I could see, other than a cut on his neck and a nasty looking sore on his ear. It breaks my heart to think about what goes on over there."

Melvin put his arm around her and kissed her on the temple as he said "I know, Honey."

October 5, 1968 Amy Tobias walked slowly home from school with a knot rising in her stomach.

It was 4:30 on a Friday evening. She had stayed after school to help Mrs. Marcus dust the chalkboards and clean up the paint, brushes, and other supplies left laying around from art class. She would have stayed longer if she could, but it was time for her teacher to go home and the janitor had to lock up the building. She tried to think of something else to do before she went home, but it would be dark soon and she couldn't put it off any longer.

"Okay, just breathe. Breathe," she said to herself and walked the last two blocks home.

Harry was already home when Amy got there. She opened the door and stepped into a recurrent bad dream. Marcia was screaming at her husband, face red, neck muscles bulging.

Harry was standing against the love seat, balancing, trying not to fall into it. Marcia raised her palm and shoved it in Harry's face, pushing him down into the thick cushion, putting him in a more vulnerable state. He tried to rise but she kept pushing him back down, mocking him with her cruelty. She then reached to the end table for a heavy, green, glass ashtray and lifted it.

Amy screamed, "MOMMY… NOOO"

Marcia turned, as if startled by Amy's presence.

"You! What are you doing here? Do you want some of this too, you little bitch?"

"No Mommy, STOP IT. NOW."

Watching this with her own eyes was just too much for Amy.

Marcia swung and made Amy the target for the ashtray instead of her husband. It skipped off Amy's skull. She slid down the door, her mind blinking out like a blown light bulb. It was the first time Marcia had ever hit Amy, but it didn't faze her one bit. Harry stood immediately to come to his daughter's aide, but the Monster turned her bulk toward him again, and pounded on him for a while longer.

It was dusk in late winter as Amy stepped off of the SEPTA bus, one block from her home, talking excitedly with her best friend, Vera about going to college in the fall. They would be going to separate schools, but that was okay. Vera was going to Penn State, Amy was happy to say she would be getting away from her parents, out of this city and going to the University of Virginia. They said their goodbyes and Vera turned to her left to head to her home and Amy went right toward her house.

She was so wound up thinking about getting away that the anxiety about going home hadn't gotten to her. She just amused herself with happy thoughts as she made the turn onto her street. She noticed something moving within her peripheral vision, but didn't think much of it at first. *Probably just a dog, peeing on the mailbox.* But it was too large and pink for a dog. She turned, squinting into the gloom to see what it was. She saw a round, pale face down low as if a person was crouching and peering at her from behind the blue U. S. Postal Service box. The pink figure got up, ran and hid along the alley wall. *OmyGod! That was my mother!* This was an unexpected turn of events. Marcia ran again then hid behind some steps. *She's naked!* Her mother peeked above the steps, then back down, as if she was playing peek-a-boo with Amy.

"Mommy, what are you doing?" Amy said out loud, but to herself, *be verrry careful here.*

Four houses down from where Amy stood, Mrs. Kershner looked out her door and called, "Amy, I didn't know what to do so I called the cops, they should be here any minute."

"Okay, thanks." *Sure, now you call the cops, but when she's practically killing my Dad, no one bothers to call them.*

She moved slowly closer to her mother, trying to figure out her best move, when she heard the sirens approaching. The red and white patrol car pulled behind her and two uniformed officers got out.

"What's the problem?" asked the driver.

"It's my Mom, something's wrong with her," Amy said, while she was turning toward her door. "I need to go in the house and get her something to wear."

She ran into the house and grabbed Marcia's long trench coat.

"Just what every fashionable flasher wears," she laughed to herself as she fled out the door and down the steps.

The officers were cautiously approaching Marcia as she backed away, sliding along the brick wall.

"It's alright Ma'am we're here to help," the heavy cop spoke softly with his palms facing her as he followed her.

"Stay back you piece of shit, don't you come near me, if you touch me, I'll kill you."

The coldness in her voice caused both officers to slow their steps for a second, they could tell that she wasn't armed (where would she hide a weapon?) but she was big and apparently up for a fight. She could be on drugs, or drunk, who could tell with these types?

Harry noticed the red lights twirling before he drove around the corner toward home. His first thought was, *Oh, please God, don't let it be Amy, if she hurt my little girl again, I'll kill her myself.*

Relief flooded him when he saw his daughter, standing in the street, looking down toward the dead end, with a long coat draped over her arm. She turned when his headlights swept over her. He parked quickly and stepped out of the car.

"Daddy, its Mommy! She's gone nuts or somethin', she's naked. I have a coat,"

Some neighbors were peeking out their windows now, and others were just arriving home from work. *How much more embarrassment are you going to put us through, Marcia?* Harry thought. To Amy he said, "Everything'll be alright." *Will it? Will it really? Is it ever alright?*

The police crept slowly closer to Marcia then as if a silent signal was given, they pounced on her. It took a lot of pushing and shoving before they brought her mass to the ground, but they did.

"GITOFFME YOU BASTARDS.... I'LLKILL YOU I'LL FUCKING KILL YOU BOTH," she screamed, followed by a bunch of unintelligible sounds and gurgles as she fell to the ground, scraping her exposed flesh.

One cop struggled to hold her as the other pulled her arms around her back, and squeezed on the cuffs. It took both of them to pull her to her feet. Some of the fire seemed to have dissipated with the fight, but her wobbling walk made it very difficult to steer her to the car. As they led her toward the back seat, Amy rushed over with the coat, and after being granted permission, wrapped it around her mother's shoulders.

"Where are you taking her?" Can we follow you?"

"We'll be taking her to the Episcopal Hospital for some tests; you can meet us there, but I don't think they'll let you see her, but I'm sure they want to ask your father some questions."

The cop nodded in Harry's direction as he said this. He recognized him from the many emergency calls that he and fellow officers responded to over the years. He was an accident prone man, wink, wink, nudge, nudge.

Harry stood in the middle of the street dumbfounded. Fights and screaming he was used to, this he was completely unprepared for. He followed Amy to the car; she took the keys from him and pointed to the passenger side door.

"I'll drive," she just shook her head and sighed when she realized that he didn't resist or even ask where they were going.

After hours in the waiting room of the psychiatric ward, a woman in a white coat walked through one of the double doors situated about halfway down the hallway.

"Hi. I'm Dr. Green. I've examined Marcia and have some things to discuss with you Mr. Tobias. Would you follow me, please?"

"I'd like my daughter to come, too."

"Are you sure?"

"Yes"

"Okay then, both of you this way please," she led them through the doors that she had just exited and to her office, third door on the left.

When they had passed the first door on the right, Harry looked in a small window and saw his wife in a hospital gown, sitting on a cot, arms shackled to the wall. It broke his heart to see his wife chained like an animal. It reminded him of his prisoner-of-war days.

Harry and Amy sat on one side of a large desk, with the doctor on the other, as she gave them her assessment.

"I believe that Marcia needs serious help. She seems to be suffering a psychotic episode, which I haven't determined the reason for yet. I would like to have her signed into the mental institution for more tests and observation. Mr. Tobias, I'll need your signature in order to do that."

"Well...I don't know if I can do that..she'd kill mm...uh.. I'm not sure what she'd do..." he shook his head and stammered.

"In my professional opinion, I do believe it is for her own good. She's fighting and threatening people and she is very dangerous. I cannot release her like this. "

Harry looked at Amy with a confused look, "They have her chained up in there."

"Daddy, you saw her out on the street tonight, she needs help, please sign Daddy. You know what she's like, it could help you too. Daddy, please?"

Her pleading had the effect she had hoped for. He signed.

Amy stopped to admire the wreath hanging on the front door before she went inside. Harry rose from his chair, and gave her a kiss on the cheek.

"Amy welcome home, it's so good to see you. How was your first semester at college?"

"Merry Christmas, Daddy. I'm havin' a great time. Oh, and I'm learnin' stuff, too" she laughed as she wrapped her arms around him. "I see you haven't decorated the tree yet. It smells good though."

"I was waitin' for you. I brought the lights and balls down from the attic, so we can get started any time you want. You hungry?"

"No I'm fine. How's it been around here?"

"Well quiet, but I'm gettin' along."

A quiet Christmas was just what Harry and Amy needed. They decorated the tree together. On Christmas morning they opened presents, in the afternoon they cooked a feast for two, and had the best day they ever had in their home.

One day, they took a long walk in the snow to do some shopping on Fifth Street.

"Daddy, do you remember when I used to think this was "Fish" Street?"

He laughed, "That wasn't all that long ago really."

She laughed back, "Yes it was."

They didn't waste a lot of time missing Marcia. They hardly thought about her at all. New Year's Eve was celebrated in front of the T.V. watching the ball drop, while eating a variety of appetizers, and then to bed shortly after. Christmas break ended too quickly.

"Well, Amy, I hate ta see ya go so soon, but I know you have ta get back to school," Harry tried to avoid tearing up. "Take care a yourself."

"I will. I love you and you take care, too," she gave him a tight hug, let go, and turned to go before she changed her mind.

Marcia sat in the lounge of Byberry Mental Hospital, fuming about that day's visit with Harry. She demanded once again that he get her out of this place. *Stupid ass signed me in here and he could get me out.* But, from past experience she knew he was too dim-witted to handle the situation. It was time to take action. She quit taking those drugs they handed out like candy. They made her fuzzy-headed. She was going to get out on her own, no matter what it took, and who she had to kill. *Extra bonus points if it's that whore, Dr. Little Miss Know It All Green.*

Complacency was going to be her greatest ally. Security was lax. There was no such thing as security cameras in that hell hole in those days and, *They think we're all doped up and sitting here like marshmallows.* She had been watching all the comings and goings around this place and had a good idea of when to make her move. At 6:00 p.m. there was a change of shifts, and since it was winter it was dark by then, that's when she would take her chance. She was fully dressed under her filthy bathrobe, *They treat us like animals in here,* and ready for the street.

She wandered slowly down the hallway at about five minutes until six, even swayed a little to appear drugged. Nice touch. But no one noticed. Even better. She hid against the wall of a dimly lit, side hallway, which was conveniently (for her) located right next to the doors leading toward her freedom. This was reminiscent of the behavior that put her there in the first place, only this time she was wearing clothes. Two psych nurses walked through the doors; they were so absorbed in their mindless conversation that they didn't even check around as they entered the hall. Marcia suspected this would be the case since she had been watching for flaws in their system and there were many. Marcia slipped through the doors before they even started swinging shut. Too easy.

On previous occasions, Marcia had asked Harry for details on where the hallways led and how many locked doors he had to come through. She always made the questions seem like casual conversation, but she was really working on her master plan. She knew there was only one locked door, but many hallways and that she was on the third floor. She slipped quickly into a ladies room, shrugged off her robe, tossed it into the trash can and buried it under a mound of used, brown, paper towels then back out into the hallway. Now she could be just anyone, a nurse or visitor, doctor even. She walked with purpose, made herself look like she belonged on this side of the door, not the other. She made her way through the passageways and down the stairwell. *Not a good idea to take the elevator, too close, someone might recognize me.* Then out the back door, into the freshest air she'd smelled in three long years. *Waaay too easy.*

Harry made a bowl of popcorn for the movie he was getting ready to watch on T.V. and carried it into the living room. He was used to being alone now, rather enjoyed it, although he did miss Amy. He set the bowl on the coffee table, then went down to the basement and took the laundry out of the washer and put it into the dryer before the movie started. He even enjoyed these little household chores. He realized, as he smelled his freshly washed jeans, that for the first time in his life he was happy. He whistled as he climbed the wooden stairs.

The basement door was opened by a dark, hulking figure, just as the toe of his left foot reached for the top step.

"YOU LEFT ME IN THAT INSANE ASYLUM, YOU BASTARD I HATE YOU, I'VE ALWAYS HATED YOU!"

She gave him a shove and he somersaulted down the steps to the concrete floor. Harry's final back-flip caused his skull to whip back and slam against the heating unit.

Amy was beaming as she walked back to her dorm. Inside her book bag was her test scores for her final exams, all A's. This was her junior year, and at the rate she was going she could finish her education with a 4.0 GPA. She couldn't wait to tell her Dad.

She sat down to eat a sandwich in her room when her roommate, Sue Ellen burst in, "Amy the State Police are downstairs and want to speak to you, somethin' about your parents."

"My parents, again, huh," Amy said, but thought the sentence that she couldn't say out loud and would later regret thinking, *Now I know why Lizzie Borden took an axe.*

In Miami, Florida in the kitchen of their retirement home, Melvin and Anna Walsh were eating breakfast, while he read the paper. Melvin turned the page, read for a moment, got up from his chair, walked around to where Anna was seated, and pointed to a small article under *NEWS OF THE NATION*:

ESCAPED MENTAL PATIENT
SUSPECT IN HUSBAND'S DEATH

Philadelphia, Pa,

An escaped mental patient was taken into custody and charged with the murder of her husband after police tracked her back to her former home.

Marcia Tobias, 50, walked out of Byberry Mental Hospital on Friday and a search brought Philadelphia Police officers to the house on Marks Street she had shared with her husband, Harry Tobias, 52.

According to an unnamed source, the escapee was discovered in her kitchen eating popcorn and drinking beer.

During a search of the house Harry Tobias was found dead in the basement.

The case is still under investigation, but Marcia Tobias is the only suspect at this point, according to PPD Sgt. B.F. Riley.

The couple has a 21-year-old daughter currently attending the University of Virginia.

Anna read the article then sighed, "Oh, that poor man.

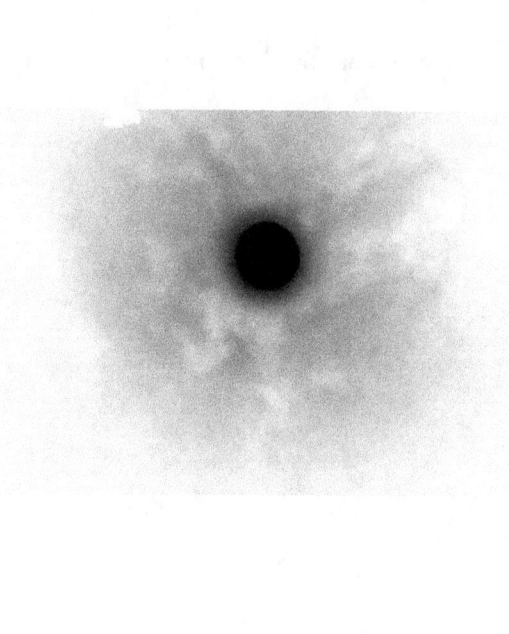

Ghosts of Sandstone Manor

I lived in a number of houses that were inhabited by spirits. All of those ghosts had been fairly powerless and innocuous. Although I have felt the presence of spirits and have heard them speak, I hadn't seen one until the summer of 2010, but that is a story for another time. This tale merges several ghost encounters from former homes with pure imagination.

Bonnie Britton came to Sandstone in 1804. She was young and pretty then. Actually she still is. She didn't live long enough to lose her beauty. She died in 1809 while giving birth to her second son, Jebediah. Although, Bonnie's body had become dust, her spirit stayed on to watch over the family. She kept a vigilant eye on her husband Buck, daughter Molly, son Peter, and of course Jeb, until he came over to her side of the world five years later due to complications of influenza.

Her spirit approved when Buck brought home a new wife to take care of their children. She understood the necessity of it. Children need a mother. She didn't quite see why he chose Carrie Walters, though, a little on the horsey side and not too smart but that was probably why she was still available at the ripe old age of 20.

Carrie's lack of intelligence was what caused the cabin, which Bonnie and Buck had built with their own hands, to burn to the ground late one night. No one else but Bonnie witnessed how the fire started. After bringing in a load of firewood, Carrie used turpentine to remove pine tar from her hands. She then hung the oily rag on the peg beside the stove. That peg was great for drying damp towels or jackets, but it was far too close to the radiating heat to hang flammable chemicals on.

Bonnie tried to warn Carrie, then Buck, before the fire got out of control, but she failed to get anyone's attention. However, it was discovered that night that Jeb had a knack for getting the attention of those still in the realm of the living. Around one in the morning, when the household was sound asleep, the blaze began. Jeb shouted at what would have been the top of his lungs, if he still had lungs. Buck was aroused by a sound he couldn't quite identify. Actually he didn't want to identify it. He then smelled smoke, opened his eyes and saw it swirling in the air. Buck leaped to his feet and ran out of the bedroom, dragging Carrie by one arm, while shouting for his kids to get out of the house. Although, the incident shook everyone up, the family was unscathed.

Jeb was delighted with his new-found skill. He perfected it over decades, practiced it and fine-tuned his technique throughout time. At first he just made noises, teased pets and farm animals, then Jeb learned to move objects around, simple things like sliding dishes across the table, or turning knobs to unlatch doors. Bonnie never developed any special communication skills; she just remained an amused observer of Jeb's practices throughout the decades.

She silently supervised as her survivors built a house of sandstone. The stones were cut from the hills above the home and slid on ice and snow by mules to the construction site. The structure was far more spacious than the original two-room log house, consisting of two stories with fireplaces in all four rooms. It was a fine home which the Brittons were rightfully proud of, and they named it Sandstone Manor.

Bonnie was pleased by other changes the family made to her home place over the years. They added a brick section to the house and laid hardwood floors cut from trees that had matured on the land. Cherry was used to install mantles, stairway trim, and handrails.

The lady spirit's young ones grew to be productive adults. Peter farmed the land beside his Pop. He married Mary Ellen Martin, which Bonnie thought was a good match, and fathered two sons, Walter and Daniel. Molly married the minister of the Baptist Church in Marshall Grove and raised four little ones of her own.

Buck and his wife passed away in time leaving the land to Peter who eventually passed it on to Walter and his young wife Laura.

The road in front of the manor was a stage coach route. This house became an impromptu hospital in 1860 when a horse drawn carriage was forced to stop because three of its passengers had come down with bumps and rashes. The driver left these three behind and continued on with his remaining travelers as these symptoms developed into pus-filled lumps, and smallpox arrived via the mountain pass. Out of reverence for the sick, Jeb was uncharacteristically quiet while the patients lie in the beds set up in the living room. He abstained from whispering into the patients' ears as he did so often to healthy slumbering visitors. Out of respect for the dead as the three succumbed to their illness, Jeb discontinued taunting and haunting the family dog. For a few days anyway. It was by some small miracle the Brittons remained healthy.

Bonnie stood silently beside Rebel soldiers in the spring of 1862 as they carved their names and rank into the soft, gritty, reddish tan stone of the exterior walls of the home. Every now and then the military horses nickered and threw their heads up; wide-eyed with fear. The reason for the spooked behavior could not be explained by the soldiers as they rehydrated with cold, clear spring water Laura offered them. It was Jeb, of course. The spirit boy growled and roared as he leaped in front of the saddled, mounts with arms flung wide. The confusion on the soldiers' faces made Jeb double over with laughter. Bonnie indulged in a chuckle or two, as well.

One-by-one Brittons were entombed in the ever-growing family plot. Some of the family members lived long lives and several did not. Farming accidents, various illnesses, hunting mishaps and natural causes claimed them, yet, for some inexplicable reason, no other relative joined Bonnie and Jeb in the nether world.

The property was sold to Patrick and Constance Kelly in 1922 by a Britton descendent when he tired of the country life. The land came with the sandstone house, barns and storage buildings, 100 acres, mineral rights and, of course, Bonnie and Jed. There was no extra charge for the latter two; their existence wasn't even disclosed in the sales contract.

Friends and family came to visit and party with the Kellys. Jeb and Bonnie enjoyed the Roaring Twenties by swirling, unseen, between dancers doing the Charleston, Fox-trot and Shimmy. Jeb entertained himself and his mother by pulling on the undulating fringe on the lady dancers' short dresses. The women just believed one dance partner or another was responsible for the tug.

Radio was introduced to the household and the sounds of comedy shows and news broadcasts could be heard reverberating throughout the halls of the manor. However, the party atmosphere was dampened by the end of the decade following the stock market crash. Although the Kellys huge garden prevented the food shortage that the Great Depression brought with it, there was a pall over the nation, and Bonnie could not help but notice the change.

The 1940's brought World War II and the Kellys said goodbye to two sons, Paul and Robert. Paul never returned home, he was shot while drifting down during a parachute drop over Germany. Robert didn't come back to the farm either; he relocated to New York City after the War, met and married Maggie, and eventually raised four children.

Sandstone Manor was never the same after Paul was lost and Robert moved away. Jeb's teasing nature was disquieting to the grieving parents. By this time he had begun speaking to the living by imitating flesh and bone humans. This became an especially fun hobby but it took many decades to accomplish.

Jeb had been mimicking Paul's voice for several years before he took his fateful trip to Europe and continued after Paul was gone. Maybe he felt he was keeping Paul alive, or perhaps he was just being cruel, but Jeb started to talk to Pat and Connie using their son's deep manly voice instead of the sound of the five year old boy he would remain for all eternity.

"Mom. Dad. Come into the living room." Jeb said in Paul's intonation and inflection.

As Constance, Patrick and their Border Collie, Tipper, walked toward the closed living room door with caution and curiosity, it opened with a click and the hinges screeched apart. The room stayed very cold even with a roaring blaze in the fireplace. The rich, warm color palette and crackling logs could not provide the warmth intended, nor could the hottest midsummer afternoon. This was Jeb's favorite room and he made himself known.

Although, Pat and Connie would not find any sign of Paul in the frigid room, Tipper could see a presence. The collie jumped onto the sofa, barked and leaped with jaws snapping at air. Tipper was after Jeb's bobbing, orb floating above the piano, over the window frame, now the mantle.

The Kellys began to shy away from the cold living room, but it was not the only area Paul's voice would be heard. Connie and Pat eventually grew used to hearing the sounds of Jeb/Paul, and it was this son's voice 73-year-old Constance heard as she took her last breath in the bedroom she shared with her husband.

"Mom, don't worry, I am waiting for you," Jeb whispered into Connie's ear using Paul's voice. This murmured encouragement eased her passing.

Patrick grieved away the next 8 months of his life, and followed his wife and Paul into the cemetery plot on the land of Sandstone Manor.

After his grandparents died in 1971, Michael, Robert and Maggie's oldest son, joined the country-wide back to the nature faze, followed John Denver's refrain,

Take Me Home, Country Roads, and moved his wife Delores and three girls out of New York City and down to the farm.

The teen girls, Karla, Kara and Katy, had no trouble with culture shock; they filled the barn with horses and the coop with chickens. Piglets ran wild in the pen and hutches were quickly overrun with bunnies. The farm animals brought out a maternal instinct in the young ladies who worked hard at cleaning and feeding. The only chore they didn't like was getting up to walk the two mile gravel road to catch the school bus each morning.

Katy often felt as if she were being watched as she did her math homework, sat in bed reading her *Little House on the Prairie* books, or even while she undressed. And, of course, she was being watched. Jeb developed a crush on the 13-year-old Katy. She was aware all too often of unseen eyes, cold sensations and chill bumps on her neck. When Michael or Delores' voices came out of the kitchen when the girls were parentless for an evening, Katy knew the sounds emanated from an unearthly source.

Although these ghostly occurrences were unsettling at first, Katy learned Jeb meant her no harm. The eternal five-year-old began speaking to Katy in his own voice and she began responding to him. Jeb became a secret confidant to the youngest Kelly and, after decades, he finally experienced a one-on-one relationship. Katy's parents and sisters just assumed the murmured conversations from behind her closed bedroom door or the stall of her horse, Beldar, was odd, but simply thought the girl was putting on the faked voice of an imaginary friend. Katy, realizing she was too old for pretend pals, just smiled at the notion, and kept Jeb's existence under wraps.

In April of 1974, the cherry trees lining the road dressed in pink, and the pear tree wore white to accentuate Karla's lacy, gown on her wedding day. The affair was held in the field behind Sandstone Manor. Kara and Katy wore orchid taffeta and carried bunches of wild flowers harvested from the hayfield and entwined with satiny, deep purple ribbons.

Bonnie and Jeb found the window in the upstairs hallway of the brick section of the house to be the perfect spot to watch the big event. Lou Carlisle, the tuxedo clad best man, admired the home as the groomsmen waited for the wedding march to begin. His scanning eyes grew wide as he looked up at the second story window. Lou's mouth dropped open and he appeared as if a chicken bone was stuck in his throat. Jeb and Bonnie gasped and leaped behind the damask curtains. It was a gut reaction at being caught in the act of betraying privacy. Had the two spirits been seen for the first time since their deaths? No one had every acknowledged seeing the apparitions before. It was just inconceivable to Bonnie and Jeb that they could be visible to live humans.

Lou would not accept the image his eyes were transmitting to his brain. It couldn't possibly be the spirits of a woman and little boy standing in the window. He didn't believe in ghosts. He wasn't drunk. Yet. But this image was accompanied by a prickling sensation at the back of his neck. As the bride began to make her way toward the groom, Lou shook off the "hallucination" and dismissed the sighting as a trick of clouds reflecting on glass, or the shadows of the huge elm tree in the yard. But, still, they looked so real.

At the risk of being discovered Bonnie and Jeb joined the reception, they did love to dance after all. To most of the guests, Katy appeared to be dancing alone, but Lou could see the small ethereal partner circling around her body. To drown out the sight of the ghosts, the best man began downing one glass of rum punch after another in an attempt to dull the images of Katy and Jeb, and the woman spirit sweeping past him in a blurred swirl of whiteness. Alcohol began to affect his judgment as it so often does.

"Are you seeing ghosts?" Lou asked Kara, Michael, the Kellys neighbor, anyone who would listen.

"You're drunk," they said.

"Yes, I know, but...." Lou stammered.

After about an hour, Lou was so sufficiently bolstered by alcoholic strength that he approached Katy.

"Are you dancing with a ghost boy?"

"I don't see a ghost boy," Katy said with a coy smile. And she was answering the question honestly, she couldn't see Jeb, but she knew he was there.

"You must be drunk," Katy teased as she rolled her eyes, and danced away with Jeb spinning beside her.

Not drunk enough to stop apparition sightings, Lou stumbled off, and headed to his car fishing keys out of his pocket. Kara snatched the keys from his hand, steered him to her own vehicle and drove him home. This gesture grew into a romance, and Lou and Kara wed two years later. Lou never talked about the ghosts he saw in her parent's house and avoided visiting there as much as possible.

Katy continued her friendship with Jeb until she was accepted to UCLA. To wish farewell to the new student, Katy's final day at home was celebrated with a barbeque and bonfire. Before bed, Katy tried to explain to the anxious spirit boy that she would visit him during breaks, but Jeb became inconsolable at the thought of her leaving him behind. After several hours of a futile discussion, it was time for Katy to get sleep before her early flight to the west coast.

As Michael, Delores and Katy slept, Jeb stormed about the house throwing things. Bonnie shushed him and spoke softly trying to calm her son. She followed him outside. He headed for the dying bonfire with its glowing, pulsating remnants. Unfazed by the hot, smoldering limbs,

Jeb began tossing burning sticks onto the porch. One of the twigs landed on a party streamer and a flame flared up. Bonnie became frantic and insisted Jeb wake the Kellys. He refused. He smiled at the fire as it curled up the strip of party paper until it reached the porch roof. Jeb looked demonic as his eyes reflected the flames red glow. The Kelly family slept on.

By midnight, the fire slipped between the window frame and glass panes. Around 1 o'clock, the den furniture began blazing. Bonnie once again compelled Jeb to scream; he ignored her and watched the fire grow stronger. The Kellys continued to sleep. As 2 AM neared, the fire became a conflagration and Katy was awakened by a burning sensation in her nose and throat. She immediately realized her home was on fire. In one leap she was out of bed, in the next step she was in the hallway. Her parents met her there and they raced hand-in-hand down the burning staircase. At the bottom of the steps they ducked beneath flaming beams, and navigated through blazing furniture and over fiery carpet.

The Kelly's escaped the crumbling house, but their home would not survive. The three stood before the blaze, helpless to stop the destruction. Sandstone Manor was eight country miles from the nearest volunteer fire department, too far away to possibly hope fire fighters would arrive in time to save the house. Michael shook from loss and frustration. Delores cried. Katy listened for any sign of Jeb. Where is he? Why didn't he wake her? He had told her the story of his family and the log house. Why hadn't he shouted for her to get up? Where were he and his mother? That answer came in the form of smoke shaped like a woman and a smaller, smoky human form rising above the caving roof. This was the first time Katy saw Jeb and he was swirling up and away comingled with smoke from the house fire. The humanoid shapes rose until they dissipated and blended into the night's dark clouds.

Although a new house was built with resurrected bricks from Sandstone Manor, Bonnie and Jeb did not supervise the construction. They did not occupy it once complete. They no longer witnessed the lives of subsequent families, nor did they dance, tease and play. Jeb and Bonnie were gone.

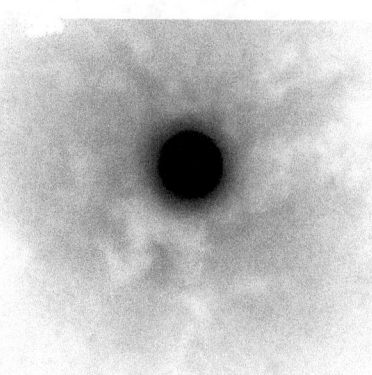

Things Break

I'm not sure of the actual science behind telekinesis or psychokinetic energy, or whether there is a link to puberty, but I have experienced unexplained energy movements both positive and negative during certain times of the month. For humor's sake I developed this story that I feel many women can relate to.

Things started breaking around the time Charlotte Morris began puberty. Her psychokinetic phenomenon was nothing compared to what a pig blood dripping, teenage girl demonstrated before her taunting peers on prom night. Charlotte certainly didn't have the awesome power of the little fire starter. No, her telekinetic ability was more of a disability. An irritating curse.

To complement Charlotte's mood swings, cramps and tampons, clocks stopped ticking and television reception grew fuzzy. As the years went by, Lottie's problems grew steadily worse, although no connection was made for a long time.

A golden, teenaged Charlotte enjoyed sharing yard work with her father, Joe. Time spent cutting brush, weed pulling and garden planting was bonding time for Lottie and Dad.

Joe turned the key of the riding mower to the off position, climbed out of the seat and sauntered toward the white house to take a sip from his glass of iced tea perched on the edge of the porch. Charlotte threw her long, slim, legs over the mower's platform and plopped into the seat.

"You can't hog the mower all day, it's my turn now," Lottie shouted and grinned.

As she turned the key, the small engine sputtered, gears screeched and Charlotte cringed, "Oh, that didn't sound good."

Joe walked toward the lawn tractor, "It was running fine a minute ago. Hum. Let me try."

Charlotte stood to the side as Joe took the seat and flipped the key to the right. The mower's motor started without a glitch. Joe set the break and climbed off.

"Okay Lottie, try again."

No sooner had her butt hit the pleather, when the motor choked on its own noxious fumes and died.

"I'll be damned," Joe said.

Charlotte stepped down and Joe tried again. The engine started immediately. Lottie and her father shrugged as she turned to get the rake to gather the grass already sheared from its stems and roots.

The same type of thing happened with her car the day Charlotte took her driving test. An excited Lottie sat behind the wheel of the late model Honda Civic with Wally, the examiner, in the passenger seat. With a long reach, Wally pulled to stretch the seat belt across his ample belly.

"Okay, Charlotte, start her up and drive into the lane."

Lottie tried to oblige as she turned the ignition, but like the mower, the engine would not fire. She tried again and again but only felt the car rocking from side to side accompanied by a knocking sound from under the hood followed by a stalling engine. Knock, stall. Knock, stall.

"Looks like you flooded it. I can't just sit her until you quit fooling with this car. I've got other drivers to test." Wally was getting a little testy himself as he opened the door and got out of the Honda.

The vehicle started immediately for Joe and he drove his disappointed, puzzled daughter home. Charlotte took her test two weeks later and walked out of the department of motor vehicles with temporary license in hand.

Time keeping became another challenge. Each month, the hands on Lottie's watch began to spin around the dial at twice the normal speed for two weeks then stopped suddenly, only to return to normal 5 days later, or as soon as she unbuckled the band and set it aside. She couldn't figure out the timepiece's freaky behavior but discontinued wearing a watch.

Cooking a meal during her monthly visits became frustrating since each time Charlotte pressed the microwave's start button, or turned on the toaster oven, the power went out.

"Uggghhh," Charlotte groaned as she made her way down the dark steps and through the black basement to the breaker box.

One would assume this was an electrical wiring problem, but it never happened when her parents cooked, or during any of Lottie's other physical states.

Throughout her college years, computers in the study hall went awry and the screens froze up whenever Charlotte walked past feeling crampy. Yet the same computers operated normally once there was some distance between her and the computer towers. This occurrence did not go unnoticed by her classmates who began referring to the condition as the Lottie Virus.

Charlotte's condition caused quite a stir in church the Saturday afternoon she acted as maid-of-honor for her college friend, Mary. As Lottie was escorted up the aisle by the best man, Rob Marlow, statues lining the walls began to tip and topple as guests leaped up to steady the falling religious icons. This was bad enough, but when the two arrived at the front of the church, candles upon the altar began to fall over. Several tapers ignited small flames along the lace runners on the altar which were quickly extinguished before the wedding march began.

The guests weren't sure what to make of the episode, but several people made sideways glances and eyed Charlotte suspiciously as if to wonder if she were one of Satan's disciples. Lottie began to wonder if she was going to be burned at the stake before the evening was over but the night finished without such a dramatic event.

The candle flames were not the only sparks that caught during the wedding and reception. Embers grew within Lottie and Rob while dancing. They spent all night following the ceremony talking and getting to know each other.

They fanned the romance for several weeks before consummating the relationship. Lottie and Rob's first sexual encounter was incredible. The two melded and morph together as one flowing, pulsating form of positive energy. They climaxed simultaneously and explosively that night and most every time afterward.

Rob and Lottie's personal relationship followed the same exciting course as their sexual one. Their personalities made a beautiful tapestry when woven together. Most of the time.

A strange incident in the grocery store gave the couple a fun story to tell and retell at parties. As Charlotte and Rob wandered down an aisle searching for items on their shopping list, the husband and wife circled opposite sides of baked bean cans stacked one on top of the other in a six foot high pyramid. As Lottie walked close to the display, the cans in the center of the triangle shoved backward toward Rob and barely missed shattering his ribs.

The cans of baked beans seemed to attack Rob, or were maybe attempting to escape Lottie's energy. Bean cans at the top of the triangle tumbled, spun, crashed and clattered to the floor as the tower lost the supporting cylinders beneath them.

Store clerks ran to the area to see what the commotion was all about. Rob and Charlotte began laughing so hard they couldn't explain that neither of them had physically touched the display.

Odd phenomenon like that happened often enough to add interest to their marriage. But it was more serious repercussions of Lottie's strange cycles that prevented the couple from having an incredible marriage all the time instead of most of the time.

One such repercussion of her bizarre condition developed as Charlotte and Rob began to plan a family. During her ovulation, Rob mysteriously became impotent.

"It's okay, these things happen. Maybe it's the pressure of becoming a father," Charlotte assured her husband.

"No, I'm not the least bit worried about having kids. I look forward to it. I just don't know what is going on," Rob said.

The rest of the month returned to splendid, sexual normalcy for the two, but each time they tried to make a baby, Rob could not stay firm.

After years of fervent, yet unsuccessful, attempts Lottie and Rob grew restless. The strain began to take a toll on the marriage and Rob's manhood. He began to stray. He was always able to perform during his many affairs, so much so that he became a father with another woman. This ended what would have otherwise been the marriage others dream of.

Lottie had a number of romances following the divorce, but oddly they shared Rob's condition during Charlotte's frustrating state. But as she neared her 50th birthday, fewer things broke, including parts of the male human anatomy, vehicles, computer components, and all objects that operate on electrical impulses. As she aged, her telekinetic rampages wound down.

Lottie was a beautiful older woman. Her golden hair was intertwined with silver and she maintained her slim, long legged stature. Despite the AARP card in her wallet she still attracted the attentions of men, particularly younger men. When most woman grow less desirable, Charlotte Morris became more so.

It was not unusual to see Lottie drive down the street with a hot young guy in the passenger seat, or watch her dance the night away with a different man twenty years her junior. Although her neighbors referred to her as a hussy for her many vibrant relationships, she preferred to be called a cougar. Whatever term she was known as, Charlotte enjoyed every explosive minute of it.

Forever Caged

This is not exactly a true story; it is based on my experience in the same circumstance as the reporter in this tale. Although I was not the recipient of the horrible visions I wrote about, I had a strong feeling that if I had stayed in the lock-up area for much longer I would certainly become a victim of these phantom sensations.

It is another typical Southern West Virginia large, brick, building with tall white columns, built in the 1700's with a similar history behind it, once a stage coach stop, a military school, a hospital known for its healing sulphur waters, now a newly remodeled hotel waiting for guests. *Writing this newspaper article for the state fair edition will be a cinch*, or so I thought, as I snapped an exterior photo.

Although the day was cloudless, the ancient structure looked slightly dark and ominous sitting on the hill, but that was more because of its aura and not a matter of shadows. These historic places have stories to tell and not all of them as bright and sunshiny as the weddings which occur on a regular basis at these beautiful settings along the Greenbrier River.

I crossed the massive porch then entered one of the double doors. There was a stack of brochures in a wooden stand on the check-in counter; I took one of the pamphlets which contained the historical background of the place. A huge dining room was on my right and I peered through the archway. Large windows surrounding the space were draped in lily, white fabric, the tables were covered in equally snowy linens. After hearing clinking sounds coming from a door in the opposite wall, I entered the room and followed sounds of tinkling glass. In the kitchen, I introduced myself to a harried, Fred Batiste, the owner of the hotel, restaurant and spa, loading a large dishwasher.

"The staff has not arrived yet and the rooms are vacant at the moment, but feel free to wander the halls, take pictures, then meet me back here when you're finished. I'll try to answer any questions you may have," Fred said, as he took a dish towel and wiped a rivulet streaming down a blank, pale swatch between two fuzzy, brown mounds atop his head.

"Thanks, see you in awhile," I replied, left the stuffy room, climbed a set of spiral stairs to the second floor and felt happy to be on my own. I can be very sociable, but on that day I preferred to discover the mysteries of the old building alone.

I walked the garishly carpeted, wide corridors between hotel rooms thinking the décor was a little too reminiscent of Stephen King's Overlook Hotel in his novel *The Shining*. I peered from time to time into the peep holes set in the doors. It is highly unusual to have peep holes that can view the inside of a hotel room, rather than out of the room into the hall, but as the brochure explained these view points were for security in the days of the military school, and later, for a women's correctional institute. There had been, according to the pamphlet, a modesty flap installed inside to cover the hole for the modern day visitor. Though I peered through a tunnel, my impression of the rooms was that the accommodations were cheery enough. I traipsed the silent hallways of the second floor, circled around and up more stairways to the third then fourth floors. All the rooms were locked.

I perused the brochure as I walked, occasionally snapped a picture or two as I finished wandering the fourth and final floor containing hotel rooms. At the end of this last hallway was an even narrower set of spiral stairs which, the pamphlet informed me, would lead to the upper level that still has prison cells from the building's correctional facility days, and a window where the confined women could watch local softball games once played in a field below. *Cool.*

I squeezed, circled and climbed feeling slightly claustrophobic. My head rose into a large, mostly empty, attic. The fact the area was mainly empty was not unusual, but what was odd was what was stored in the space. Resting among a few typical boxed storage items was a large monument wreath, a dress store dummy and a coffin. Maybe all of these things were kept at the ready for Halloween, but the coffin was not decoration quality, it was real. I had managed to keep a disquieting feeling at bay for most of my solitary tour. I have personally sensed and heard the presence of ghosts, spirits, and/or entities of another plane, so I don't spook easily, but I was beginning to experience a deeper, creepy, prickling feeling at the sight of the coffin. Despite this edginess, I ambled to an open door at the other end of the long attic. Before I entered the tiny room I could see the game-watching window on the opposite wall.

I headed straight to the framed, glass pane to gain perspective over the landscape on which the hotel sat. I envisioned the long ago games below, mentally hearing the ball hit the bats, the cheering of those in the small stands, and watching fielders scramble, and the runners sprint around bases. These sights and sounds must have been what the well-behaved female prisoners were rewarded with during summer afternoons. The not so well-behaved captive spent her time with stimulation of another sort. But as it were, terms "well-behaved," or "not so well-behaved" was a matter of interpretation by those men holding the batons, handcuffs and keys.

Before turning from the window, I felt pain - emotional, physical and mental torment - wafting toward me. I looked over my left shoulder to get the first glimpse of the tiny cells bolted to concrete walls. There was a bumpy, mattress-covered cot in one of the cramped cages. Although the correctional facility had been moved long ago, the bed was not in a state of decay. With one step, I was in front of the opened barred door to this cell. Without a conscience effort I was inside this cell. And, with the force of a hurricane driven wind, I was shoved onto the inadequately covered, hard, grating springs of the cot and the harsh clank of metallic bars rang in my ears, as the cage slammed shut behind me.

I screamed and tried to rise from my prone position to see who had pushed me and closed the door. I was able to turn around but not sit up for I was being held by unseen hands. There was no one there! The attic and most of the hotel was empty except for Fred Batiste many, many floors below. My wasted scream went unheard and I knew from experience any further cries would fall on deaf ears. Not *my* experience, mind you, but that of those who were locked in these cells before me. I am a firm believer that justice must prevail and that people need to be punished for certain acts, but the punishment must fit the crime. Some of the women who were held in those cells could not have deserved the cruelty they suffered at the hands of the guards. I was in the hotel that day to share a history about the building, but the former prisoners had a story to share with me.

Hold her down. Hold her down. I mentally heard the gruff voice and smelled foul breath blown by warm air. My struggles were useless against the two or three invisible entities in the cage. Although the guards were illusionary, the pressure of their brutish hands on my arms, neck and shoulders felt all too real. So was the searing pain as a number of items ranging from sharp, blunt, jagged, round, square and every other shape within easy grasp of my sadists, were inserted deep into my body cavities.

Just as suddenly as they appeared my tormenters were gone and the pain left with them. All that remained was the image. With shaky hands, I tried to open the cell door but it was still locked. I rattled the cage and screamed for the hotel owner but my voice was lost in the empty hallways between us. As I looked around for a prying tool, the cage door snapped open.

The mental slide show had only just begun. I felt a presence, but this time there seemed to be only one man. This apparition was a kinder spirit. Coldness seeped through my physical body as it was consumed with the presence of another and this spirit felt drawn to this gentle guard. The entity, using my body, allowed this man to hold, kiss, fondle, and make, quick, but pleasing, love to the ghost inside me. I felt every thrust, heard every groan and murmur before it ended and my own blood flooded out the chill the spirit brought with her.

As time passed, I experienced brutal bludgeoning, starvation, dehydration, gang rapes, and the feeling of raw sores from chains wrapped around my wrists and ankles for extended periods. I was once again inundated with the spirit that loved the guard, and this time I felt a life growing inside my womb which brought a small amount of pleasure to this horrid environment. But despite the warden turning a blind eye to the everyday torture, he could not allow this child to be born. How possibly was he to explain that condition? So he sent in a termination crew with batons in hand. While handcuffed to the cell bars, I was beaten about the stomach. Not being content that battery of the abdomen would do the trick, my soiled uniform and underwear was ripped away and a broom handle was forced inside my body. With the stick's extraction I felt the life and the prisoner's spirit wash out of me.

When I stood, the ghost of the woman who occupied my form was standing beside the window. I walked out of the open cage and looked out the glass pane to follow her pensive gaze. She pointed to the prison garden, green with leafy vegetable plants, and I could hear her unspoken words. *That is where they bury the aborted fetuses. I have several hidden there, and there are many more. Too many to count.*

I turned away, ran the length of the attic and scurried down the spiral staircase. I passed a room with the door left ajar. *That door was closed when I went up to the attic. Don't look inside. Don't look inside.* I raced down the other sets of stairs and out the front door into the sunlit afternoon. I didn't stop to ask Fred Batiste any questions. I had more answers about the building's history than I ever wanted to know.

About The Author

Theresa Flerx was raised in Philadelphia, Pennsylvania, and moved with her family to West Virginia when she was sixteen years old.

After marrying a radio talk show host, they traveled back and forth across the country, living in New Jersey, Virginia, Massachusetts, California and Michigan.

After divorcing in 2001, she earned an associate's degree in Criminal Justice/Law Enforcement with a 4.0 GPA, and was named in the National Dean's List. She is working toward her bachelors degree and beyond.

While training at the Sacramento Police Academy, she sustained an injury which ended her aspirations of becoming a police officer.

Theresa once again makes her home in West Virginia. She worked for several years as a reporter for the West Virginia Daily News when she won the 2006 Best Photography News Award from the West Virginia Press Association Better Newspaper Contest.

She is a freelance writer of on-line articles.

Visit her website at www.tflerxanecdotalist.com for short stories, regular blog and information on upcoming books.

Also by Theresa Flerx

Disequilibrium and The Multi-Facted Crystal Ball, a true life story of insanity, deception and murder.

www.ingramcontent.com/pod-product-compliance
Lightning Source LLC
Chambersburg PA
CBHW071333130626
46556CB00004B/1872